Edgar Allan Poe
STORIES BY POE

essay by
Gregory Feeley

ACCLAIM BOOKS
STUDY GUIDE

Stories by Poe

art by H.C. Kiefer, Jim Lavery and Rudy Palais
adaptation by Samual Willensky and John O'Rourke
cover by Jen Marrus

For Classics Illustrated Study Guides
computer recoloring by VanHook Studios
editor: Madeleine Robins
assistant editor: Gregg Sanderson
design: Scott Friedlander

Dale-Chall R.L.: 8.6

ISBN 1-57840-028-7

Acclaim Books, New York, NY
Printed in the United States

STUDY GUIDE

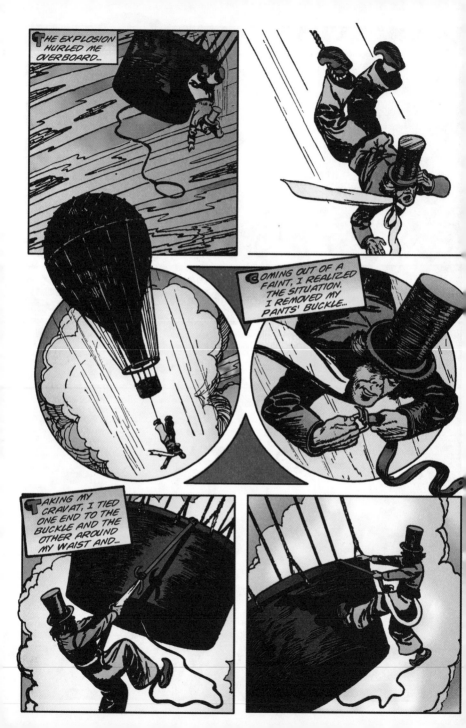

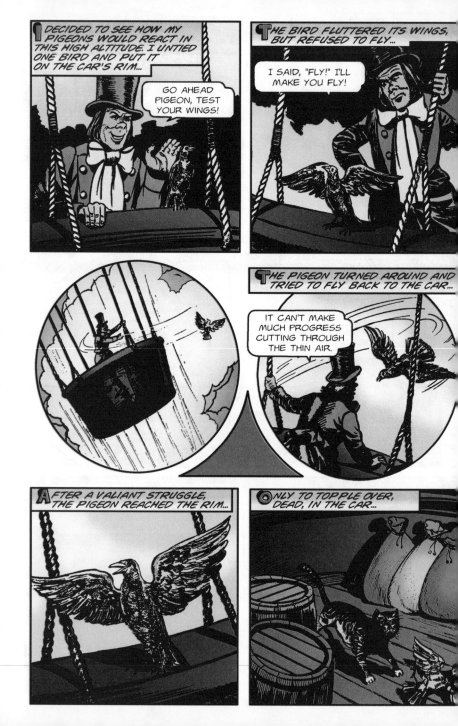

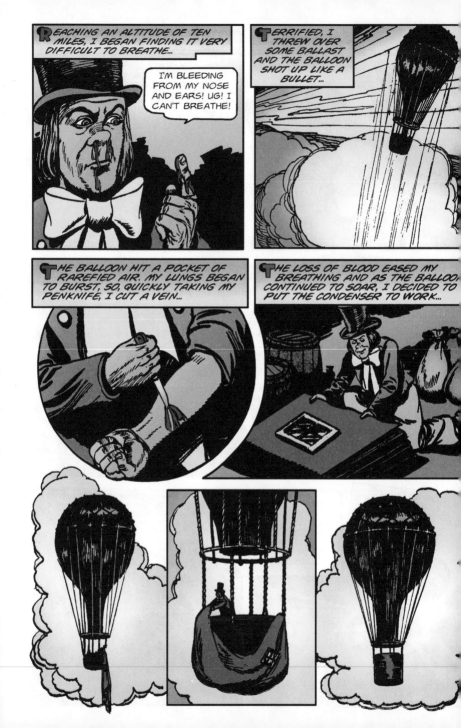

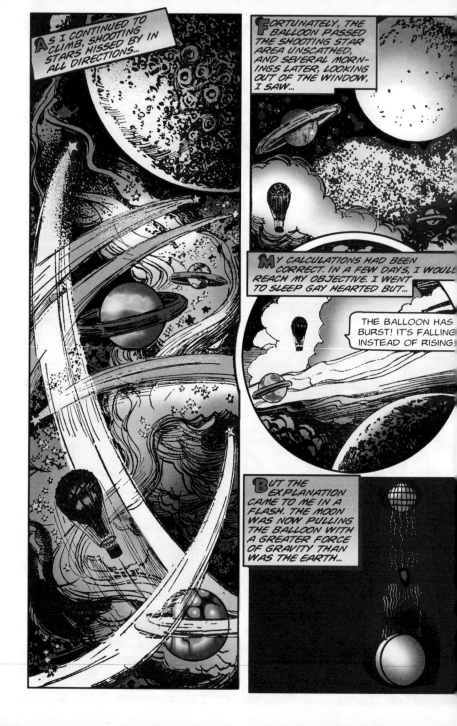

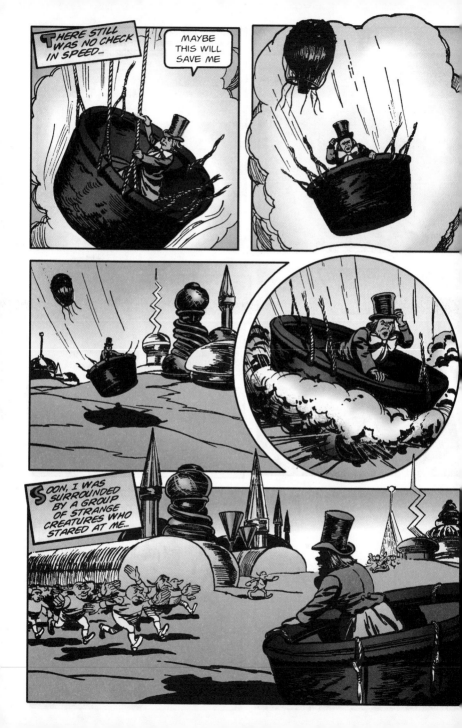

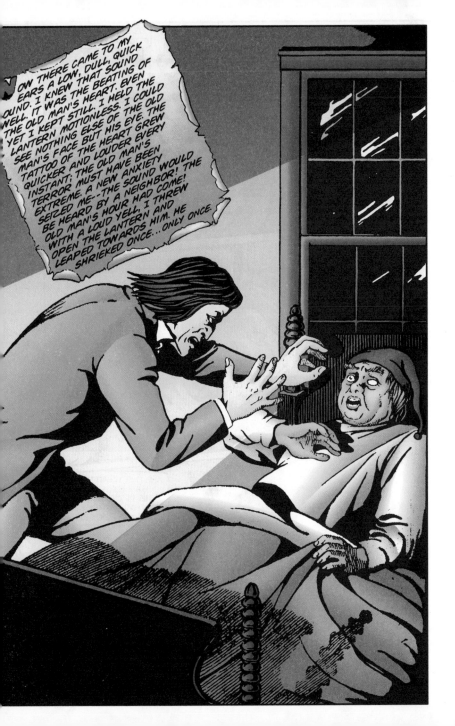

ITHIN THE WALL THUS EXPOSED BY THE DISPLACING OF THE BONES, WE SAW A STILL INTERIOR RECESS, IN DEPTH ABOUT FOUR FEET, IN WIDTH THREE, IN HEIGHT SIX OR SEVEN. IT SEEMED TO HAVE BEEN CONSTRUCTED FOR NO SPECIAL USE WITHIN ITSELF, BUT FORMED MERELY THE INTERVAL BETWEEN TWO OF THE COLOSSAL SUPPORTS OF THE ROOF OF THE CATACOMBS.

STORIES BY POE
EDGAR ALLAN POE

Edgar Allan Poe was born on January 19, 1809, in Boston, Massachusetts. His parents were professional actors, a rather disreputable profession in the 19th-century, and when Poe's mother died before his third birthday, he was brought up by a friend of his mother's family, a stern Scottish tobacco merchant who lived in Richmond, Virginia.

Although as an adult he lived in such northern cities as New York and Boston, Poe would always consider himself more of a Southerner than a New Englander.

For various reasons—perhaps because of the early loss of his mother, perhaps because his Scottish foster father did not share Edgar's sensitivity, perhaps because of the insecurity he apparently felt at being the son of actors—the young Poe grew to adulthood with a lifelong insecurity, which often took the form of rash, even self-destructive behavior.

At the age of sixteen Poe became engaged to Elmira Royster, his childhood sweetheart, despite the strong objections from both families. The next year he entered the University of Virginia, but his foster father refused to support him, and he was forced to withdraw a year later for lack of money. He returned home to discover that Elmira's family had been intercepting his letters to her, and had forced her to marry another man.

Devastated, Poe left for Boston, where he attempted to make a living for himself. Finding this impossible for a seventeen-year-old who wished to make a career in literature but had not completed college, he entered the army. Sometime afterward he published his first volume of poetry, at the age of eighteen.

Two years later Poe resigned from the army and enrolled at West Point for officer training. Although he was popular with his fellow students and excelled in his classes, Poe soon realized that he was not cut out for a military career. When his foster father refused to sign his release papers, Poe intentionally disobeyed orders (mostly by refusing to show up at chapel and roll call) and was expelled. His fellow cadets, however, donated the money that permitted him to publish his second volume of poems.

With no prospects, Poe moved to Baltimore, where he lived with his paternal aunt and her eight-year-old daughter Virginia. He submitted five stories for a contest being sponsored by a Philadelphia newspaper. Although none of them won, the newspaper published all five. Though still poor, he was now a published poet and story writer.

A year later, in 1833, Poe submitted stories and poems to another contest, and one of the poems won second place in the poetry competition, while his story, "MS. Found in a Bottle," won the $50-first prize for fiction. This was enough for a family to live on for a few weeks. The next year Poe published a short story in a national magazine, and began to write a series of book reviews, which earned him the nickname "Tomahawk Man" for their cutting wit. Although they helped found his reputation as a brilliant writer, they also made him numerous enemies.

At this time Poe also began to edit various magazines. Although he was an innovative and respected editor, he was very badly paid, and he continued to live in conditions of near-poverty. The aggravation this caused Poe's naturally nervous temperament drove him to occasional bouts of excessive drinking, which his enemies cited to blacken his reputation.

In 1837 the twenty-seven-year-old Poe married his cousin Virginia, shortly before her fourteenth birthday. Neither marriage between first cousins nor marriage to a girl not yet past her mid-teens was terribly unusual at that time, although it strikes us as bizarre today. Edgar and Virginia were extremely happy together, but remained poor, and Poe lived in constant anxiety. Nonetheless, he managed to write a steady stream of essays, stories, and poems.

When Virginia was nineteen she became ill with tuberculosis, which left her a near-invalid. The following years, during which Poe wrote many of his most famous works, were marked by extreme poverty and unhappiness. Although he became famous as the author of "The Raven" and various stories, and enjoyed a great reputation in France, he was never free of financial worry. At one point Poe went to Washington in order to be interviewed for a minor position in the administration of President Tyler, but he got drunk and ruined his chances. His own health began to break down, and rumors (almost certainly false) spread of his taking drugs.

In 1847 Virginia died, and Poe fell gravely ill. He eventually recovered, resumed writing, and in 1849 he returned to Richmond, where he met his old love Elmira Royster Shelton, now a widow. They became engaged, and at the end of September Poe returned to New York to set his affairs in order. He stopped in Baltimore, where he evidently engaged in a binge of drinking and collapsed. He died a few days later, at the age of forty.

POE'S WORK AND INFLUENCE

Although his career lasted only twenty years, Edgar Allan Poe created a large and varied body of work: his collected writings (which don't include his work as a maga-zine editor) come to seventeen volumes. (This alone is enough to rebut the charges that he was a drunkard or drug abuser.) Nearly all of what he wrote came in the form of short pieces: poems, stories, articles. He only wrote one novel, *The Narrative of Arthur Gordon Pym*, and only a handful of long stories. Most of his stories are quite short: many of the best are less than ten pages long. Poe's inclination toward brief works is in part a result of his work as a magazine editor, but it also reflects his beliefs in the poetic and symbolic nature of literature: in an era when fiction tended to be long and discursive (the most famous novelist of Poe's day was Charles Dickens, whose books were routinely more than 800 pages long), Poe wanted fiction to aspire to the condition of poetry: every word carefully chosen, their final arrangement formal and concise.

Poe developed a theory of fiction that exalted the short story as the only literary form besides the poem where "the highest genius could be most advantageously employed for the best display of its own powers." Poe was not interested in simply telling a good story, but in creating what he called "the unity of effect or impression." Different types of literature were appropriate for different kinds of effects. Although "Beauty can be better treated in the poem," the short story is best for evoking such emotions as "terror, or passion, or horror." He explains:

"A skillful literary artist has constructed a tale. If wise, he has not fashioned his thoughts to accommodate his incidents; but having conceived, with deliberate care, a certain unique or single *effect* to be wrought out, he then invents such incidents—he then combines such events as may best aid him in establishing this preconceived effect."

Poe's archaic language makes this a bit hard to follow, but it is clear that he isn't interested in the "tale" as a mere sequence of actions that hold the reader's attention. What we call "dramatic tension" held no interest for Poe; he was not trying to write a page-turner that keeps the reader wondering what is going to happen next.

This is surprising when we consider Poe's reputation for macabre tales. Edgar Allen

Poe—who wrote about premature burials, monstrous obsessions, disastrous voyages, and prisoners subjected to diabolical tortures—was not particularly interested in narrative suspense? Modern horror writers from Stephen King to Harlan Ellison have written of the enormous impact Poe had on them as young readers, when poetical effects don't count for very much and the ability to tell a good story counts for everything. However Poe set about to write his fiction, his final effect could indeed induce the "terror, passion, or horror" he desired.

THE ADVENTURE OF HANS PFALL

"The Unparalleled Adventure of One Hans Pfaall" (the full title) was one of his earlier stories, published in 1835 when the author was twenty-six. He had previously written only one of the stories for which he is remembered today: "MS. Found in a Bottle" is—like "The Adventure of Hans Pfall"—an explorer's narrative. Much of the world was still unexplored by Westerners in the first half of the 19th century—Africa was still known as "the Dark Continent," and the Arctic and Antarctic regions remained mysteries to science—and stories of travel to an unknown land, especially traveling by balloon, remained popular throughout the century.

Hans Pfall's destination, however, isn't a lost continent or uncharted island, but the Moon. Lunar voyages had excited the imagination of European writers for hundreds of years—travel to the Moon by implausible means such as being towed by a flock of geese or flung by a giant spring—but Poe's carefully described voyage of a trip in a balloon seems to be the first story that actually made an attempt to describe how such a journey might be possible.

Hans Pfall carefully calculates how long it will take him to reach the Moon at a speed of sixty miles an hour, and takes into account the fact that the higher one ascends from the earth, the thinner the atmosphere becomes. (Poe was unaware that a balloon cannot ascend through the vacuum of space, and didn't realize that his "aeronaut" would experience zero gravity upon leaving the orbit of the Earth; but his attempt at scientific authenticity was unsurpassed until Jules Verne wrote *From the Earth to the Moon* thirty years later.)

Poe is known almost exclusively as a dark and macabre writer, but "The Adventure of Hans Pfall" is one of his rare humorous stories. Pfall's Dutch countrymen are described with satiric strokes—in addition to the comical names such as "Rubadub" and "Underduk," the supposed Dutch propensity for pipe-smoking to excess is gleefully described—and Pfall's trip to the moon (in a balloon made of dirty newspapers) is motivated not by the spirit of adventure or scientific curiosity, but in order to escape his creditors.

It is interesting that Pfaall shares his creator's financial anxiety, and that he goes to great lengths to revenge himself upon his tormentors—just as Montresor, the narrator in "The Cask of Amontillado," is later to do. The narrator of "The Tell-Tale Heart" also finds himself compelled to kill someone he finds intolerable, although vengeance is not *his* motive. Despite its light-hearted tone, "The Adventure of Hans Pfall" demonstrates Poe's ability to dramatize states of gleeful, almost insane malice.

The Character of Hans Pfall

Although Hans Pfall is first seen in a situation of financial awkwardness, he never shows a moment's self-doubt or despair, not even when he is considering suicide. His self-confidence concerning the feasibility of

WOMAN SPECTATOR RECOGNIZES THE FLOATING HAT...

THAT HAT BELONGS TO MY HUSBAND HANS PFALL! I'D RECOGNIZE IT ANY PLACE!

his invention, and his self-satisfaction over his ingenious means of blowing up his tormentors, are the only most obvious signs of an enormous personal assurance. In this respect Hans Pfall resembles another famous traveller who made a home for himself after being thrown up on a strange land: Robinson Crusoe. Poe's protagonists are often tormented, usually by circumstances more psychological than material; but those of his protagonists who look outward at the world rather than inward at themselves tend to be self-possessed and successful.

There is only one time when Hans experiences a strong emotion, and that is when he is thrown from the balloon and finds himself hanging by a rope caught round his ankle. Poe describes vividly the horror Hans feels when he becomes aware of his situation:

"It is impossible—utterly impossible—to form any adequate idea of the horror of my situation. I gasped convulsively for breath—a shudder resembling a fit of the ague agitated every muscle and nerve in my frame—I felt my eyes starting from their sockets—a horrible nausea overwhelmed me—and at length I lost all consciousness in a swoon."

This feeling of absolute terror as one realizes he is in a situation of unspeakable menace is one which Poe evokes repeatedly through his work, particularly in stories like "The Tell-Tale Heart," and "The Pit and the Pendulum."

GOODBYE DEAR FRIENDS! I HOPE BY THE GREATEST OF MIRACLES, YOU REACH EARTH SAFELY.

Even here, however, Hans does not dwell long on his awful plight, but instead sets out immediately to remedy it. When he recovers consciousness, he uses the tools he has available to him—his belt buckle and his cravat—to regain mastery over his environ-ment. From this point on, Hans experiences not a moment's anxiety or doubt: he conducts experiments with his pigeons and kittens, makes calculations, and observes the wonders of space. In the CI edition, we see him weep for the lost kittens, but in Poe's version, Hans merely watches the basket fall and thinks that "My good wishes followed it to the earth, but, of course, I had no hope that either cat or kittens would ever live to tell the tale of their misfortune." Hans Pfall is an adventurer, not a sentimentalist: Poe's characters can be analytical, demented, or terror-stricken, but they are never sentimental.

THE TELL-TALE HEART

"The Tell-Tale Heart," one of Poe's most famous and terrifying stories, was first published in 1843. By this time Poe was an accomplished writer, and the story shows him with his powers fully developed. In its vivid depiction of the consciousness of a madman, this concentrated and very short story (only five pages long, compared to "Hans Pfalls"'s more than fifty pages) creates an unforgettable impression. Most murder stories are filled with details of the crime, but "The Tell-Tale Heart" is stripped of everything but the bare essentials. We don't know the narrator's name, his age, or his relationship to the "old man." The location and era in which the story takes place are ignored: nothing but the stark details—a man obsessed with the thought of killing his harmless benefactor—are set before us. Of the old man, we have no detail of his appearance save for his single blind eye, "the eye of a vulture—a pale blue eye, with a film over it." These grotesque features, in the absence of any other description, become our sole image of the old man.

In "The Tell-Tale Heart" we have nothing but the narrator's testimony—his voice, speaking to us from we don't know where (the final panel of the CI adaptation, showing him wearing a straight jacket in a padded cell, represents the artist's guess as to his fate—Poe never actually tells us). The entire story takes place inside the narrator's mind, which raises an obvious question: If all you know is what one of the characters says, how can you be sure what is true?

This question goes to the heart of Poe's tale. The narrator declares that he is sane in the very first sentence, even as he admits to being "very, very dreadfully nervous." Anyone who begins a narrative by insisting on his sanity (and going on about it for another few paragraphs) is going to provoke immediate suspicions in the reader. We are, in fact, in the presence of a madman, one obsessed by the notion of his sanity, and who begins his account by admitting "I killed the old man." This means that we are in for an unusual reading experience: just as the words "Once upon a time…" are a signal that we should listen to, and believe, what is to come, the opening words of Poe's narrator warn us that we should *not* trust what is to follow.

Even before we fully understand the situation that the narrator is so eager to explain, we notice that his style of speaking is as alarming as what he is actually saying. "Object there was none. Passion there was none. I loved the old man. He had never wronged me. He had never given me insult." Poe's prose style is generally rather fancy—look at the long, elaborately constructed sentences and the formal vocabulary in "Hans Pfall"—but the narrator here is speaking in short, staccato sentences, as

though the turmoil he feels is too great for him to frame anything longer. If it isn't the style of a madman, it is at the very least the style of a deeply disturbed one.

Then the narrator begins to explain why he *did* want to kill the old man. At this

point all doubts concerning his insanity vanish. "I think it was his eye! yes, it was this!…Whenever it fell upon me, my blood ran cold; and so by degrees—very gradually—I made up my mind to take the life of the old man, and thus rid myself of the eye forever."

There are two points to note. The narrator obsesses over aspects of the old man's body: he fixates upon the old man's blind eye, just as he shall later fixate upon his beating heart. It's this that convinces us that he is indeed insane. But what is even more alarming is the fact that the narrator is making up his mind even as he speaks: he does not know why he killed the man until he muses aloud on various possibilities right in front of us. Although most of the narrative covers past events, at times we see the narrator's mind in the present tense—in the act of speaking to us—swerve this way or that.

When this presentation of an insane mind is not shocking, it can be grimly comic. "Madmen know nothing," he boasts. "But you should have seen *me*." The narrator's monstrously incongruous actions seem at times darkly funny, whether we mean to laugh or not. When he describes the absurd slowness with which he sticks his head into the sleeping man's room, then says, "Ha!—would a madman have been so wise as to do this?" We are indeed liable to think "Ha!" though not for the reason he imagines.

The narrator's bizarre actions continue even after he has conceived and carried out his horrific murder. The old man dies with the heavy bed lying on top of him, after a protracted period of extreme terror. Very likely he died of fright; even had he been suffocated, there would be no sign of foul play on his person. Yet the narrator does not simply return the old man to his bed, where he can claim to have found him dead the next morning—instead, *he dismembers the body in a tub*, then buries the pieces beneath the floorboards of that very room. This is perhaps the worst thing he could do, yet he brags of his wisdom.

What follows is one of the most remarkable moments of horror in all of Poe's fiction. No sooner has the narrator completed his efforts at concealment than there is a knock at the door. Three policemen are there to investigate. The narrator welcomes them, invites them to search—indeed, to "search *well*," and even ("in the enthusiasm of my confidence") offers them a seat right in the room where the murder had taken place, with the narrator sitting directly upon the spot where the dismembered corpse has been hidden.

At this point, at his moment of supreme triumph, the narrator begins to experience symptoms of distress. He feels pale, his head aches, his ears ring, and as the symptoms grow more acute, he realizes that the ringing comes not from within his ears, but from elsewhere in the room. Within seconds the narrator realizes that what he hears is the beating of the old man's heart, which is steadily growing louder. His frenzy of alarm—in which he finally is convinced that the policemen *must* be hearing it as well, and are pretending not to only in order to torment him—is a moment of extraordinary intensity, more horrific even than the murder that preceded it.

Plot Analysis

What actually happens in "The Tell-Tale Heart"? The narrator's account of the events is one we can rule out almost immediately: whatever this extraordinary story is about, it is *not* a tale of supernatural horror, with a murdered man's heart continuing to beat in the grave. As every reader understands almost immediately, the narrator imagines the terrible heartbeat: Poe plainly means us to realize that the narrator would have gotten away with his crime had the consequences of his mental instability not overtaken him.

"The Tell-Tale Heart" is, then, a story of psychological horror. The narrator describes events that *seem* fantastic, but prove (upon the reader's reflection) to be the products of his own tormented psyche. Poe explored this theme repeatedly in his stories and poems, most famously in "The Raven,"

in which a grief-stricken man imagines that a bird who flies into his study is a messenger from "the Night's Plutonian shore"—the land of the dead where his lost love may reside.

So there is no ghostly retribution in "The Tell-Tale Heart"; the ruin that overtakes the murderer is brought on by his own overwrought imagination. Is that all there is to the story—a tale of an insane murderer whose insanity proves his undoing? No; and to appreciate fully Poe's complex and powerful tale, we must peel back the successive layers of mystery.

What is the relationship between the narrator and the old man? (See next page.) We are never told, but some of the story's peripheral details allow us to make a guess. No one else lives in the house, otherwise the narrator would have been unable to murder and dismember the old man uninterrupted. The narrator is a younger man (since he calls his benefactor "the old man"), and evidently lacks wealth, which the old man possesses in abundance.

He might be a servant, but the fondness the old man displays for him (and which he reciprocates) seems to argue against this. Could he be the old man's son?

This is entirely possible. Even a son who is acknowledging paternity can refer to his father as "the old man," and the narrator's refusal to give any details of their relationship suggests that he is denying the extent of their closeness. He says nothing of how he came to live in the old man's house, and one possible reason is surely the fact that he has never lived anywhere else.

If the old man cannot be shown conclusively to be the narrator's father, he is certainly a father-figure; the early 19th century, with its high mortality rate, was full of stepfathers and relatives raising nieces and nephews—Poe was himself raised by a foster father (with whom he quarreled!). But even this detail isn't so important: what matters is that the old man functions in the story as a paternal figure: protective, unconditionally loving, giving shelter in his home.

So why does the narrator develop a murderous resentment against his father-figure? Because, he says, of the old man's eye, which he later calls his "Evil Eye." The evil eye is a familiar element from folklore: an eye whose gaze can inflict deliberate harm. The "vulture eye" is probably blind—it has a film over it, and the old man doesn't react when the beam from the narrator's lantern falls upon the opened eye—but it's consistent with the mechanisms of superstition that the eye that lacks normal powers may possess supernatural ones.

Yet why would the old man harm the narrator with his "Evil Eye"? "He had never wronged me," the narrator admits. If he fears the magical powers of that blind eye, it isn't because it is about to do him evil—indeed, he calls it "the Evil Eye" only after

HE NEXT DAY, I WAS VERY KIND TO THE OLD MAN...

HERE, MY FRIEND, GIVE ME THE BROOM. I'LL DO ALL THE HOUSE WORK TODAY. YOU JUST REST.

I'M GLAD YOU'RE HERE. YOU'VE MADE A FINE COMPANION FOR MY LONELY OLD AGE.

AND YOU'RE A FINE OLD FELLOW YOURSELF.

he has begun to elaborate his self-justification. If a blind eye has a feared magical power and it isn't the power to do evil, then it must be the power to see *better* than normal vision.

It's at this point that a possible motive becomes clear. If the old man was the narrator's father or stepfather, then his gaze becomes the stern watchful eye of the parent upon the child. The child's fear that a parent's all-seeing gaze will catch him out in some forbidden act can be a terrible one, and more resembles the narrator's unspecified horror at the gaze of his loving benefactor than anything about an actual "Evil Eye." If the narrator cannot tell us what it is he fears about the eye, it is because what he fears being caught doing is too shameful to express aloud, even to himself.

This possible interpretation—that the narrator has, in some sense, killed his own father—carries strong echoes of the most famous parricide in literature, the murder by Oedipus of his father, the king. In Sophocles' drama, the murder of the father is, in fact, closely connected with the theme of sight and blindness. And while we know virtually nothing about the old man (save that he is master of his house), what few details we do get are images that liken the old man to a king. And the way the narrator buries the old man within the confines of his own house (indeed, in his own chamber) seems to equate the man with his domain, as though they were king and realm.

Poe knew the play *Oedipus Rex* well; he alluded to it more than once in his critical writing, and once wrote of the playwright's "obscure and terrible spirit of predestination, sometimes mellowed down towards the catastrophe of their dramas into the unseen, yet not unfelt hand of a kind Providence, or overruling God." The catastrophe of the drama that overtakes the narrator and the old man seems indeed the product of "an obscure and terrible spirit of predestination," but no overruling God (Poe means here one of the Greek gods, not the Christian God) shall mellow down its horrible nature.

We don't have to accept this interpretation in order to appreciate the psychological terror of the universe the tormented narrator inhabits. The house's windows are shuttered closed, and we know nothing whatever of the world beyond them, save that the old man's single scream was enough to alarm a neighbor, bringing the police. Night—the period during which the old man's eye is powerless—is the only time when the narrator feels free of the Evil Eye; and he achieves this freedom only by dint of standing utterly still inside the old man's door, immobilized. And the old man is characterized only by his "vulture" eye, but the word *vulture* is repeated three times, as though to remind the reader (to say nothing of the narrator) that what a vulture looks at are creatures that are soon to die.

In destroying the old man, the narrator destroys himself: this is only the most obvious of the many associations that serve to bind together murder and victim. The narrator takes enormous pleasure in shining a beam upon the eye of the helpless, sleeping old man, reversing the persecution he imagines in the "Evil Eye"'s being cast upon *him*. When the trio of policemen appear the instant he finishes hiding the body (as though summoned by his guilty conscious), the narrator tells them that the shout which a neighbor had reported—the shriek of the

old man in the second before his murder—had been his own. And the imagined sound of the dead man's pulse, which the drives the man to a frenzy of self-betrayal, is of course the sound of his own pounding heart.

THE CASK OF AMONTILLADO

"The Cask of Amontillado" was written in 1846, three years before Poe's death. Scarcely longer than "The Tell-Tale Heart," it is one of Poe's most compressed and intense stories. "Cask" resembles "The Tell-Tale Heart" in other respects as well. Both are stories of a murder, narrated by the murderer. In each case the murder seems inexplicable to us, although the murderer considers himself amply provoked. And each murder—like several other murders in Poe's work—involve the body being concealed in the walls (or floor) of a house.

But there are important contrasts. "The Tell-Tale Heart" was told almost entirely in narration—the only times when someone speaks directly are when the old man cries, "Who's there?" and, in the final paragraph, when the murderer shrieks his confession. "The Cask of Amontillado," however, is told almost entirely in dialogue. And while "The Tell-Tale Heart" ends with the narrator's discovery and arrest, the narrator of "The Cask of Amontillado" gets away with his crime—or does he?

The action of the story is even simpler than that of "The Tell-Tale Heart"; there is only one scene, in which a single act is smoothly carried out. Montresor accosts the drunken Fortunato amid the carnival festivities, lures him into the crypt beneath his palazzo, and there revenges himself. The story does not even contain a complication: Fortunato never suspects what is happening, and puts up no fight. The narrator encounters no difficulties at any point. How can you have a story, even a very short one, where nothing happens except the completely successful execution of a simple plan that the narrator described in the opening paragraph?

One way Poe manages to sustain suspense is by his extremely rapid pacing. "The thousand injuries of Fortunato I had borne as I best could; but when he ventured upon insult, I vowed revenge." Not only does this get things off to a rapid start, but it leaves us wondering: the protagonist is more upset by one insult than by a thousand injuries? Montresor then describes the qualities that his revenge must take: "A wrong is unredressed when retribution overtakes its redresser." (In other words, he not only must take revenge; he has to get away with it.) In addition, the victim must know who did it to him.

Although we learn right away that Montresor is about to avenge himself on Fortunato, we don't know *how*; Poe wrings considerable suspense from making us wonder exactly what Montresor plans to do after he has lured Fortunato sufficiently deep into his vaults. For the rest of the story, we see Montresor play on the drunken Fortunato's vanity until the man insists on accompanying him back to his palazzo; he engages in morbid humor (when Fortunato says that he shall not die of a cough, Montresor replies, "True"; he makes the joke about being a mason. The reader, knowing that violence is very soon to come, responds to this humor with mounting tension.

The Character of Montresor

Is Montresor, who diabolically leads a supposed friend into his vaults then walls him up alive, as insane as the narrator of "The Tell-Tale Heart"? It's easy to suspect so. He condemns his companion to a horrible death for an "insult," yet we never hear about the insult. Wronged men are usually quite willing to talk about how they were wronged. Is Montresor's motivation finally as irrational as that of the old man's killer?

Poe doesn't give us any obvious answers, but he does offer some clues. When Montresor tells Fortunato that he is indeed a mason, Fortunato replies, "You?

Impossible! A mason?" Fortunato's drunken indiscretion seems to betray his low opinion of his friend. Earlier, Montresor had said to Fortunato: "Your health is precious. You are rich, respected, admired, beloved; you are happy, as once I was. You are a man to be missed. For me it is no matter." Note that Fortunato doesn't contradict these claims, even for politeness's sake: while Montresor is—like so many of Poe's protagonists—morbidly oversensitive, he isn't delusional: he overreacts wildly to Fortunato's insulting attitude, but he hasn't imagined it. Is Montresor one of Poe's few successful protagonists—a man who achieves his revenge and gets away with it? (Even Hans Pfall fails in winning a pardon for his murders.) It's true that his crime goes undetected, but has "retribution overtake[n]" him nonetheless?

Let us look at the story's grotesque conclusion. (The comic-book dramatization had to omit a few details, so this is the version as Poe wrote it.) Montresor has walled up the space where Fortunato is chained save for one last brick. At this point Fortunato, who had been screaming, utters a low laugh, which causes Montresor's hair to stand erect. They exchange a last few words, but then Fortunato falls silent. Here are the final paragraphs:

> *I grew impatient. I called aloud—*
> *"Fortunato!"*
> *No answer. I called again—*
> *"Fortunato!"*
> *No answer still. I thrust a torch through*
> *the remaining aperture and let it fall within.*

There came forth in return only a jingling of bells. My heart grew sick—on account of the dampness of the catacombs. I hastened to make an end of my labor. I forced the last stone into its position; I plastered it up. Against the new masonry I re-erected the old rampart of bones. For the half of a century no mortal has disturbed them. In pace requiescat! (See previous page)

This certainly sounds like absolute triumph; but look again. Montresor's insistence that his heartsickness is "on account of the dampness" isn't going to fool anyone. Some kind of terror has gripped him, one that—as with the narrator of "The Tell-Tale Heart"—he cannot explain to himself. He hastens to finish a job that he was previously enjoying. And while he concludes his story on the gleeful cry "*In pace requiescat!*" it is clear that *he* has not rested in peace.

Daniel Hoffman, an authority on Poe, has noted the similarity between FORTUNato's and MonTRESOR's names. Montresor and Fortunato are, in a sense, doubles—mirror images of each other. We see this when Montresor, after listening to his victim's protracted screams, responds by screaming back. Perhaps this act reminds him of their ultimate resemblance, for it is soon after that his glee is replaced by unease. In walling up his enemy, Montresor is in a sense killing himself.

in the story.

•The narrator of **"The Tell Tale Heart"** tells the reader he is not insane—and how he knows he's not insane. Is he right? What characteristics of madness does he seem to overlook?

•The narrator speaks of "the disease" he has (the one that has sharpened his senses) in the story's first paragraph, but never mentions it again. Did Poe simply forget about this detail, or does it play some part in the story that follows?

•A common interpretation of "The Tell-Tale Heart"'s ending is that the narrator is deluded by his guilty conscience into thinking that he hears his victim's beating heart. Does the narrator give signs of being troubled by guilt? Is it his undoing?

•In **"The Cask of Amontillado,"** why did Poe name his narrator's enemy "Fortunato"? Discuss other examples of irony in the story.

•The catacombs of the Montresors are filled with the bodies of Montresor's ancestors. In burying Fortunato there, what is Montresor unwittingly doing?

•In the story Fortunato wears a striped fool's costume with a cap and bells upon his head. Why is he dressed this way? What is the narrator wearing as he conducts Fortunato back to his home? Why is this significant to the story?

Study Questions

•Most of **"The Adventure of Hans Pfall"** is descriptive and unemotional, but the opening and closing moments are quite satirical. Did Poe do this on purpose? If so, why?

•How does Hans Pfall, the simple bellows-mender, differ from those dignitaries Mayor Underduk and Professor Rubadub? Is Poe suggesting something about the differences between honors and actual accomplishment?

•"Pfall" is an ironic name for Poe's protagonist, since he goes up but never comes back down. Give other examples of irony

About the Essayist:

Gregory Feeley is a critic, novelist, and contributor to the *Encyclopedia of Fantasy* and *Grolier Multi-Media Encyclopedia of Science Fiction*. His essays have appeared in *The Atlantic Monthly*, *The Washington Post*, and *New York Newsday*; and he is the author of *The Oxygen Barons* (Ace, 1990).